The Adventures of
Tom Sawyer

MARK TWAIN

STERLING CHILDREN'S BOOKS

New York

STERLING CHILDREN'S BOOKS
New York

An Imprint of Sterling Publishing
387 Park Avenue South
New York, NY 10016

"A Song for Aunt Polly"
Published 2006 Sterling Publishing, Co.
Illustrations © 2004 by Amy Bates
"The Best Fence Painter"
Published 2006 Sterling Publishing, Co.
Illustrations © 2004 by Amy Bates
"The Birthday Boy"
© 2007 by Sterling Publishing Co., Inc.
Illustrations © 2007 by Amy Bates
"The Spelling Bee"
© 2007 by Sterling Publishing Co., Inc.
Illustrations © 2007 by Amy Bates
"Too Sick for School"
© 2010 by Sterling Publishing Co., Inc.
Illustrations © 2010 by Nonna Aleshina
"Tom's Treasure Hunt"
© 2010 by Sterling Publishing Co., Inc.
Illustrations © 2010 by Nonna Aleshina

ISBN 978-1-4549-0587-5 (hardcover)
ISBN 978-1-4549-0588-2 (paperback)

Distributed in Canada by Sterling Publishing
c/o Canadian Manda Group, 165 Dufferin Street
Toronto, Ontario, Canada M6K 3H6
Distributed in the United Kingdom by GMC Distribution Services
Castle Place, 166 High Street, Lewes, East Sussex, England BN7 1XU
Distributed in Australia by Capricorn Link (Australia) Pty. Ltd.
P.O. Box 704, Windsor, NSW 2756, Australia

For information about custom editions, special sales, and premium and corporate purchases,
please contact Sterling Special Sales at 800-805-5489 or specialsales@sterlingpublishing.com.

Manufactured in China
Lot #:
2   4   6   8   10   9   7   5   3   1
06/13

www.sterlingpublishing.com/kids

Contents

CHAPTER ONE

A Song for Aunt Polly

Tom Sawyer had just eaten lunch
It was a very big lunch,
but he was still hungry.
Tom was always hungry.
He tiptoed into the parlor,
looking for candy.
He found peppermints
in the candy dish.
Just as Tom took one . . . .

Dong! Dong!
There went the
grandfather clock!
It was time for his
piano lesson,
but Tom wanted to go
swimming with his friends.

"Tom!" Aunt Polly called.
She was coming down the stairs.
Oh, no! She would be sure
to make Tom go
to his piano lesson!
He looked around.
Where could he hide?

Tom heard Aunt Polly's footsteps.
They were getting closer
and closer and closer!
Tom had to find
somewhere to hide.
The closet!
That was a good place.
He dashed inside.

Aunt Polly looked
around the parlor.
She did not see Tom—
only the cat on the sofa.
"Where can that boy be?"
she asked the cat.

Aunt Polly put on her glasses.
She still did not see Tom.
Aunt Polly knew Tom
didn't want to go to his lesson.
"Every week he tries to hide,"
she told the cat.

"I'll find that rascal.
He can't hide from me!"
Aunt Polly took a broom.
She poked it under the sofa.
No Tom.

Aunt Polly looked
everywhere for Tom.
She looked behind
the drapes.

She looked behind the grandfather clock.

She looked inside a large urn.
Still, there was no Tom.
"That boy isn't here,"
Aunt Polly said.
"Maybe he's in the garden."

In the closet,
Tom's nose twitched.
He tried to stop the sneeze,
but it came anyway.
ACHOO!

Aunt Polly threw open
the closet door.
She had found Tom!
Tom looked up.
He smiled at his aunt.
"Care for a peppermint,
Aunt Polly?" he asked.

"Tom!" Aunt Polly cried.
"Why are you in the closet?"
The piano book was in his
aunt's hand, so Tom thought fast.
"I was looking for my
piano book," he said.
"It's time for my lesson."
"That's why I was calling
you!" Aunt Polly said.
"Didn't you hear me?"
"No, ma'am," Tom said.

He kept his fingers crossed
behind his back.
"Well, hurry along,"
his aunt said,
"or you'll be late!"

Tom walked along.
He came to two paths.
One path led to
his piano lesson.
The other one led to
the swimming hole.
Tom wasn't sure
which path to take.

Then he felt the sun.
It was so very warm on his face!
He looked up at the sky.
It was so very blue!
Tom made up his mind.
It was too nice a day
for a piano lesson.
He was going swimming!

Tom met his friends
at the swimming hole.
Splish! Splash!
He jumped into the water.
He swam and played.
What a great time he had!
Tom wished he could stay longer,
but he knew Aunt Polly
was waiting for him.

Tom dried off.
He was careful to wipe up
every drop of water.
Tom thought this
was very clever.
Aunt Polly would not know
he had been swimming.
She would think he had been
at his piano lesson!

Aunt Polly was waiting
for Tom on the porch.
Tom hummed as
he skipped up the steps.
"You sound happy,"
said Aunt Polly.
"Did you enjoy your lesson?"
"Yes, Aunt," said Tom.
He crossed his fingers
behind his back.

"It's such a nice day,"
Aunt Polly said.
"Many boys would have
liked to go swimming."
"That's true, Aunt," Tom said.
"Many boys," said Aunt Polly,
"but not you, right, Tom?"

"No, ma'am," Tom said.
He crossed his fingers
behind his back again.
Aunt Polly felt Tom's shirt.
Tom knew she wanted
to see if it was damp.
He was glad he had
dried off so carefully.

"Your shirt is dry!"
said Aunt Polly.
She smiled at Tom.
"You did not go swimming.
You went to your lesson."
She kissed Tom
on the top of his head.

"Tom!" Aunt Polly cried.
She felt his hair.
It was still wet.
Tom had dried his clothes,
but . . . *uh-oh!*
He had not dried his hair!

Tom looked up
at Aunt Polly.
She was frowning.
Tom felt sad.
He had upset his aunt.
"I'm sorry," Tom said.
"Don't be angry!"

Uh-oh, thought Tom.
She was *still* frowning.
How could he
make her happy?

Then Tom had an idea.

He went inside.

He sat at the piano.

He began to play

his aunt's favorite song.

He tried not to miss any notes.

Aunt Polly stopped frowning.

She hummed a little of the tune.

Then she started to sing.

Tom soon joined in.

Aunt Polly wasn't angry anymore.

That made Tom happy.

Playing the piano was fun!

Next week, he *would*
go to his lesson.
"I promise, Aunt!" Tom said.
Tom couldn't cross his fingers
when he was playing the piano . . .
so he crossed his toes,
just in case.

CHAPTER TWO

The Best
Fence Painter

It was Saturday.
The sun was shining.
What a wonderful day
Tom Sawyer had planned!
He was going fishing
down by the river.
He got his fishing pole.

"Not so fast!" said Aunt Polly.

Tom's aunt had a bucket of paint.
She also had some brushes.

"Are you painting?" asked Tom.

"No, Tom," Aunt Polly said.
"*You* are going to paint.
You are going to paint
the fence outside.
Then you may go fishing."

Tom walked over to the fence.
How very long it was!
It seemed to go on and on.
He felt tired just looking at it.

Tom dipped a brush
into the white paint.
He painted for a bit.
His work looked good!

Then Tom looked at all
he still had to do.

"I will never finish!" he said.
How he wished he didn't
have to paint the fence!
How he wished to go fishing!

Then Tom saw his friend
Ben Rogers down the street.
Suddenly, Tom had an idea.
He knew a way to paint
the fence without doing
any of the work!

Tom started painting again.
As he worked, he hummed.
Ben walked up to Tom.
"Hello, Tom," Ben said.
"Too bad you have to work,
and on a Saturday, too."
Ben did *not* sound sorry.

Ben took a bite of his apple.

Tom's mouth watered.

How he wanted that apple!

"I'm going fishing," Ben said.

"I guess you can't come.

Not with all that work to do!"

"Work?" Tom said. "*Work?*"
"*This* isn't work to me!
I can fish any old time,
but I don't get to paint
every day, do I?"

Ben watched Tom paint.

It did look like fun.

 "*I* want to paint!" Ben said.

 "I don't know . . ." said Tom.

 "You can have an apple," Ben said.

 "Well, okay," said Tom.

Tom sat under a tree.
He ate the tasty apple.
He watched as Ben
did his chore for him.
His plan was working!

After Tom finished the apple,
his friend Billy Fisher came by.
Billy saw Ben painting,
and Billy's jaw dropped.
"That is *Tom's* fence!" Billy said.
"Why are *you* painting it, Ben?"

"I want to," Ben said,
"and Tom is letting me
because *I'm* his friend."

Billy went over to Tom.

"*I* want to paint, too," said Billy.

"I don't know . . ." Tom said.

"You can have my lollipop," said Billy.

He gave it to Tom.

Tom gave Billy a brush.

Then more of Tom's
friends passed by.
Each one wanted
to paint the fence.
Tom let all the boys
have a turn . . . as long as
they gave him a treat.

Soon Tom was stuffed with goodies
and he had painted the fence
without doing any of the work.
He was the best fence painter ever!

Tom could not wait
to tell Aunt Polly
he was done painting.
Now she would
let him go fishing!
Tom ran inside.

"May I go fishing?" Tom asked.

"So soon?" asked his aunt.
"How much of the fence
did you paint?"

"All of it," Tom said.

"*All* of it?" asked Aunt Polly.
"So soon, Tom Sawyer?
How could that be?"

"Come see!" Tom said.

Aunt Polly and Tom went outside.

"You did finish!" she said.

"I'm so pleased, Tom.

Come, I have a reward

for you, my dear."

Aunt Polly took out donuts.

"I baked these today," she said.

Tom took a big bite of one.

His tummy started to hurt.

He remembered all the sweets
he had already eaten.
He moaned and groaned.

"My tummy hurts!" he said.
So Aunt Polly quickly
sent him off to bed.

Tom saw his friends
outside his window.
They had fishing poles.
   "We're going fishing," Ben said.
"Do you want to come?"

Tom sure did,
but Aunt Polly said,
    "Sorry, boys.
Tom's tummy hurts.
He can't go fishing."

Then she gave Tom medicine.
Ugh! It tasted *awful*.

How Tom wished he had not
eaten so very many treats!
He promised himself next time
he *would* be the best fence painter—
one who didn't fool his friends—
one who painted his fence himself!

CHAPTER THREE

The Birthday Boy

Tom Sawyer ran
all the way home.
He had been fishing.
What a fun day he'd had!
Tom saw his brother, Sid,
in the front yard.
Sid was raking leaves
into a big pile.

A frown was on his face.

"Where were you?" Sid asked.

"Fishing," said Tom.

"Aunt Polly told you to help
me," Sid said. "I had to do
all the chores myself."

Just then, Aunt Polly
came down the road.
Tom hid his fishing pole
behind a tree.
"Don't tell Aunt Polly
where I was," Tom said.

Aunt Polly opened the gate.
"I see all the leaves are raked,"
she said. "What a good job.
You boys may both
have some apple pie."

Sid mumbled something.
"What did you say, Sid?"
Aunt Polly asked.
"Only I should get pie,"
Sid told his aunt.
"I did all the work!"

"What?" Aunt Polly cried.

"Tom went fishing," said Sid.

"Look, Aunt Polly!"

Sid pointed to the fishing pole.

Aunt Polly picked up
the fishing pole.
"Is that true, Tom?"
asked Aunt Polly.
Tom nodded.
"I'm sorry," he said.

"Go to your room,"
said Aunt Polly.
"There will be no pie
for you, Tom."

Tom glared at Sid.
"Tattletale," Tom said.
"I'll get you for this!"
Tom stomped off
to his room.

The next day
was Sid's birthday.
Sid was having a party.
He invited Tom.
Tom was still angry
with Sid, though.
So he decided
he would not go.

Then Tom saw Sid's
big birthday cake.
It was one of
Tom's favorites—
banana cream
with white frosting.

Tom's mouth watered.
He decided to go
to Sid's party after all.
Tom sat down at the table.

Aunt Polly brought in
bowls of blueberries.
She set a bowl
in front of each boy.

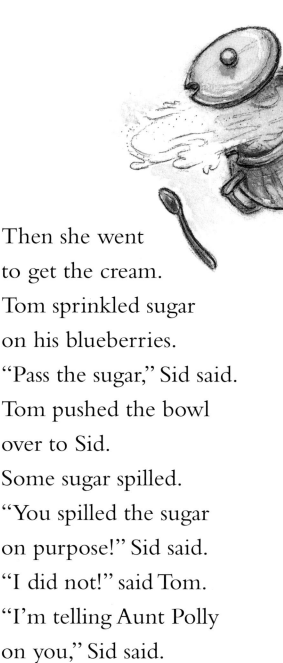

Then she went
to get the cream.
Tom sprinkled sugar
on his blueberries.
"Pass the sugar," Sid said.
Tom pushed the bowl
over to Sid.
Some sugar spilled.
"You spilled the sugar
on purpose!" Sid said.
"I did not!" said Tom.
"I'm telling Aunt Polly
on you," Sid said.

"Go ahead," said Tom,
"but pass the sugar
back over here first."
Sid gave the bowl
a hard push. . . .
Crash! It fell to the floor!

Aunt Polly came back
with the cream.
She had seen
Sid push the bowl.
She had seen it
crash to the floor.
Her nephews did not
know she had seen it.

Tom was going to enjoy
seeing Sid get in trouble
for a change!
Then Tom saw Sid's face.
It was very pale, and Sid's
eyes were very wide.

Tom suddenly felt bad
for his brother and said,
"Aunt Polly, I'm very sorry.
I broke the bowl."
"Tom, that is a lie,"
said Aunt Polly.

"I saw what happened.
Sid broke the bowl.
Now, both of you boys,
go upstairs to your room."
"What did I do?" Tom asked.
"Think about it," said Aunt Polly.

Tom sat on his bed.
Sid sat across from him.
They were very quiet.
Tom tried to figure out
what he had done.
All he could think about
was the cake downstairs.

The two brothers sat silently.
After a while, Sid said,
"Tom, I broke the bowl.
Why did you take the blame?"
"I have more practice
getting in trouble than you,"
said Tom. "I'm better at it."

"Aunt Polly says it's
not nice to lie," said Sid,
"but it was nice of you to try
to keep me out of trouble."
Tom blushed. "I guess," he said.

They sat quietly again
until Aunt Polly walked in.
"If you boys have learned
your lesson," she said,
"you may come eat cake."

Suddenly, Tom figured out
why his aunt had sent him
to his room along with Sid.
"I have learned my lesson!"
Tom said. "I was just telling Sid
that it's not nice to lie."

"That is a lie!" said Sid.

"I was telling that to Tom!"

Aunt Polly threw up her hands.

"No cake for you, Tom!" she said.

"Only Sid may come with me."

Sid started to follow his aunt.

Then he saw Tom's face.
It was very sad, and Tom's
eyes were filled with tears.
Sid suddenly felt bad
for his brother.

"Aunt Polly, I would like to make
my birthday wish now, before
I blow out the candles," Sid said.
"I wish Tom could come eat cake."
"All right," said Aunt Polly,
"if that is what you wish, Sid."

"Sid, that was nice!" said Tom,
as they all went downstairs.
Sid blushed. "I guess," he said.
"On my birthday," said Tom,
"I was going to wish for
a whole cake just for me.
Now I'm going to wish for two—
one for me and one for you!"
Sid smiled at his brother.
"That sounds fine, Tom" Sid said.
"That sounds just fine."

CHAPTER FOUR

The Spelling Bee

It was Monday morning
Time for school!
Tom Sawyer was running
as fast as he could.
He didn't want to be late.

Tom ran past
a big tree.
A sign was on it.
It said that the circus
was coming to town.

Tom stopped running.
How he wished he could
go to the circus!
Too bad he had spent
all his allowance!

The bell was ringing.
Tom made it to class
just in time.
There was a seat next to
Becky Thatcher, the new girl.
Tom hurried to sit in it.

"Hello, Tom," Becky said.
She smiled at him.
Tom felt his face get hot.
Everyone said Becky was
the prettiest girl in school.

"Hello, Becky," Tom said.
Then he buried his face
in his lesson book.

Mr. Masters was
their teacher.
"I have a surprise,
class," he said.
"We are having
a spelling bee.
The winner will get
a ticket to the circus."

The class turned
to look at Edward.
Edward was the
smartest boy in school.
He always won
the spelling bees.

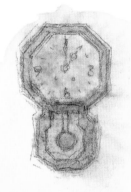

Tom looked at Becky.
Now she was smiling
at Edward—not Tom.
Right then and there,
Tom decided *he* would
win the spelling bee . . .
even if it meant studying
his spelling words!

The spelling bee was
later that afternoon.
Tom studied during lunch.
He studied during recess, too.
He studied the spelling words
until he knew them backward
and forward. Tom had never
studied so much in his life!

At last it was time.
The students stood
next to their desks.
Whoever spelled
a word wrong
had to sit down.

The last one standing
would be the winner.
Tom was so nervous,
he couldn't keep still.

Tom got his first word right.
He got his next word right.
He got the one after that right.
Soon, Tom, Edward, and Becky
were the only ones left standing.

Then it was Edward's turn.
To everyone's surprise,
he did not spell his word right!
Now it was between
Tom and Becky.
Who would be
the winner?

Mr. Masters put down
the spelling list.
"We have used up the words
on this list," he said.
"We must use a new list."
He took out another paper.
Oh, no! thought Tom.
I did not study *that* list!

"It is your turn, Tom,"
Mr. Masters said.
"Spell *circus*."
Tom gulped.
He wanted to *go*
to the circus . . .
but he could not *spell* it!

"Tom?" said Mr. Masters.
Tom gulped again.
He looked out the window.
He saw a clown walking by.

The clown was carrying a sign.
It said, "Come see the circus."
There it is! thought Tom.
That's the word I need to spell!

Tom looked around
to make sure no one
had seen the sign.
Then he said,
"Circus. C–I–R–C–U–S."
"That is correct,"
said Mr. Masters.

Then it was Becky's turn.
Her word was *cheater*.
"Cheater," Becky said.
"C-H-E-E-T-E-R."

"I'm sorry, Becky,"
said Mr. Masters.
"That is not correct."
Becky sat down.
Tom was the only one
still standing.
He had won the contest!

Mr. Masters handed
Tom the ticket.
Tom was going
to the circus!
All his friends
shook his hand.
They told him
what a good job
he had done.

Becky came up to him.
She looked very sad.
"I so wanted to go
to the circus," she said,
"but you deserve the prize.
You are a good speller."

"You were good, too,"
Tom told Becky.
She shook her head.
"I couldn't spell *cheater*,"
she said. "I bet *you* can.
You are so smart!"

Tom gulped.
He did not feel smart.
He felt awful.
He might not know
how to spell *cheater*,
but he knew what one was.

"*I* am a cheater, Becky!"
Tom burst out.
"I saw the word *circus*
on a sign outside.
That's how I won!"

Tom apologized
and gave Becky the ticket.
Tom was very sad.
No circus for him!
Plus, Becky would probably
never smile at him again!

Tom could not look at Becky
when he gave her the ticket.
"Thank you," he heard her say.
"Now I have something for *you*."

"For *me*?" Tom asked.

"Yes!" said Becky.

Then she gave Tom

not only a big smile . . .

but a big hug, too!

"What was that for?"

Tom asked in surprise.

"That, Tom," she said,

"was for doing the right thing."

CHAPTER FIVE

——◆——

Too Sick
For School

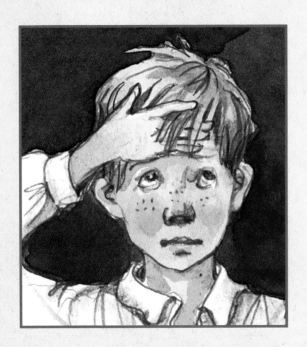

Tom Sawyer was still in bed.

He did not want to go to school.

His class had a big test.

And Tom had forgotten to study.

Poor Tom!

Maybe he could study
before school started.
Tom jumped out of bed.
He opened his schoolbook.

Tom had to know all the state capitals.

The first state was Missouri.

Tom lived in Missouri.

What was its capital?

Tom couldn't remember.

Tom dropped the book.
He climbed back into bed.
He pulled the covers
up to his neck.
If only he were sick!
Then he could stay home.

Maybe he was sick!
Tom touched his forehead.
It felt cool and dry.
He didn't have a fever.

He wiggled his fingers and toes.
Nothing hurt or was broken.
He looked in the mirror.
Was his throat red?

Tom looked some more.

Maybe his throat was a little red.

That was it!

He had a sore throat.

He was too sick for school!

Tom moaned.

He listened for Aunt Polly.

She didn't come.

He moaned louder.

She still didn't come.

Tom moaned as loudly as he could.

Aunt Polly came running
into Tom's room.
"What is the matter?" she asked.
"And why aren't you dressed
for school?"

Tom moaned again.

Aunt Polly threw her hands up.

"Oh, my!" she said.

"Don't tell me you're sick!"

Aunt Polly felt Tom's forehead.

"You're not hot."

"It's my throat," Tom said.

"It hurts."

"Let me see," said his aunt.

Tom opened his mouth.

Aunt Polly looked and looked.

"Your throat looks fine," she said.

"Are you playing a trick?"

"No, Aunt Polly," said Tom.
"My throat hurts.
But don't worry,
I can still go to school."
Tom got out of bed
and fell to the floor
in a heap.

Aunt Polly gasped.

"Young man, get back into bed.

You are not going to school today.

Do you hear me?"

Aunt Polly tucked Tom
back into bed.
Tom tried not to smile.
Now he wouldn't have
to take the test!

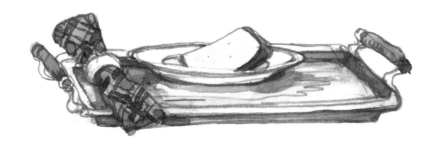

Aunt Polly brought Tom breakfast.

Tom was hungry.

But the only thing on the plate

was a piece of toast.

"Where are my ham and eggs?"

Tom asked.

"Rich food isn't good

for a sick boy," Aunt Polly said.

"Now eat up."

Tom pushed away the toast.

"Aren't you hungry?"
Aunt Polly asked.

Tom shook his head.

"You must really be sick,"
Aunt Polly said.

"Maybe fresh air will help," she said.

Aunt Polly opened the window.

"Look," she said.

"There's Doctor Robinson."

She waved at him.

"Doctor," she called.

"He's coming," she told Tom.
"Aren't you lucky!"
Tom sank lower into the covers.
He didn't feel lucky.
Not one tiny bit.

Aunt Polly went downstairs
to let in the doctor.
Tom made up his mind.
He jumped out of bed.
He got his clothes ready.

Doctor Robinson knocked
on Tom's door.
"Your aunt tells me
that you are sick," he said.
"What seems to be the matter?"

The doctor opened his bag.

Inside were many bottles of medicine.

Tom gulped.

The last time he was sick

the doctor gave him medicine.

It tasted awful.

He didn't want to take it ever again.

"I'm all better now,"

Tom told the doctor.

"And I'm late for school."

He jumped into his clothes
as fast as he could.
"I'd better have a look at you,"
Doctor Robinson said.
The doctor checked Tom's throat.
He listened to his heart.
"You are a healthy boy," he said.
"You may go to school."

"Thank you, Doctor," Tom said.
"I have to hurry now.
I have an important test."
Tom grabbed his books
and ran from the room.

At the bottom of the staircase,
Tom crashed into Aunt Polly.
"Where are you off to?" she asked.
"I thought you were sick."
"Doctor Robinson made me all better,"
Tom said.
"And I'll never be sick again.
I promise!"

Tom dashed out the door.
Class had only just started.
Tom shook his head.
As hard as it was to believe,
he was actually looking forward
to school!

CHAPTER SIX

———— ✦ ————

Tom's
Treasure Hunt

Tom Sawyer ran outside.
It was the first day
of summer vacation.
He was ready for an adventure.
But what was there to do?

He could climb a tree.
Or go fishing.
Or swim in the watering hole.
They all were fun.
But Tom wanted to
do something new.

Tom saw Joe Harper and Huck Finn
coming down the road.
He waved to his friends.
"Where are you going?" Tom asked.
"Nowhere," Joe said.
"Just walking," Huck said.
Tom joined them.

The boys walked to the river.

Tom tossed a pebble into the water.

"School is out for the summer," he said.

We should be doing something special."

"Like what?" Joe asked.

In the river was a small island.

Pirates had stayed there long ago.

"Let's row to Pirate Island," Tom said.

"What could we do there?" Huck asked.

"Be pirates!" Tom said.

"And have adventures!"

The boys packed for their trip.

Then they got on Tom's raft.

Tom gave the orders.

Joe and Huck paddled.

"Steady," Tom called out.
"Not too fast and
not too slow."
"Yes, sir!" Huck and Joe replied.

At last they landed
on Pirate Island.
Huck and Joe wanted to sleep.

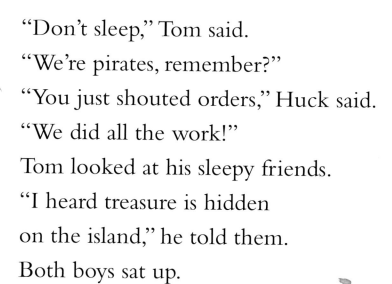

"Don't sleep," Tom said.
"We're pirates, remember?"
"You just shouted orders," Huck said.
"We did all the work!"
Tom looked at his sleepy friends.
"I heard treasure is hidden
on the island," he told them.
Both boys sat up.

"Do you think we can find it?" Joe asked.

"Not if we don't look," Tom said.

"Let's go!" Huck said.

"I'll lead the way," Tom said.

Tom and his friends walked
all over the island.
But they didn't find the treasure.
"We've looked everywhere," Tom said.

Huck pointed to a cave.

"We haven't gone in there," he said.

The cave looked spooky.
Tom didn't want to go inside.
But he didn't want his friends
to think he was afraid.
He marched up to the cave.
Huck and Joe followed.

The boys lit candles
and went inside the dark cave.
Tom walked along
a narrow path.
His candle made shadows
on the walls.
Tom's knees shook.

The path ended.

Tom stepped into a big room.

Bats flew at him.

"Huck! Joe!"

Tom called for his friends.

No one answered.

Where were they?

Just then Tom's candle went out.

Tom stood still.

He couldn't see the bats.

But he could hear their squeaks.

Tom yelled for his friends again.

"We're over here!"

Huck and Joe yelled.

Tom followed their voices.

Soon Tom saw candlelight.
He ran toward his friends
and tripped over a large rock.
"Ouch!" Tom cried out.

Huck and Joe rushed over.

"I'm okay," Tom told them.

A mark was scratched on the rock.

Tom looked closer.

The mark was a big X.

"Why is that *X* there?" Joe asked.

"To show where treasure is buried,"
Tom said.

The three boys pushed the rock aside.
Underneath was a deep hole.

Tom put his hand in
as far as it could go.
His fingers touched wood.
He pulled out a small chest.
"Pirate treasure!" he whispered.

Tom opened the chest.
It was filled with gold coins.
"We're rich!" he shouted.

Tom looked at all the coins.
"What will Aunt Polly say
when I show her our treasure?" he said.

"She'll raise your
allowance for sure," Joe said.
"I bet we'll each get a
dollar a week," Huck said.
"Think of the fun we can have
with that much money," Tom said.

Tom filled his pockets
with the coins.
Only this morning he had wished
for an adventure.
His wish had really come true!